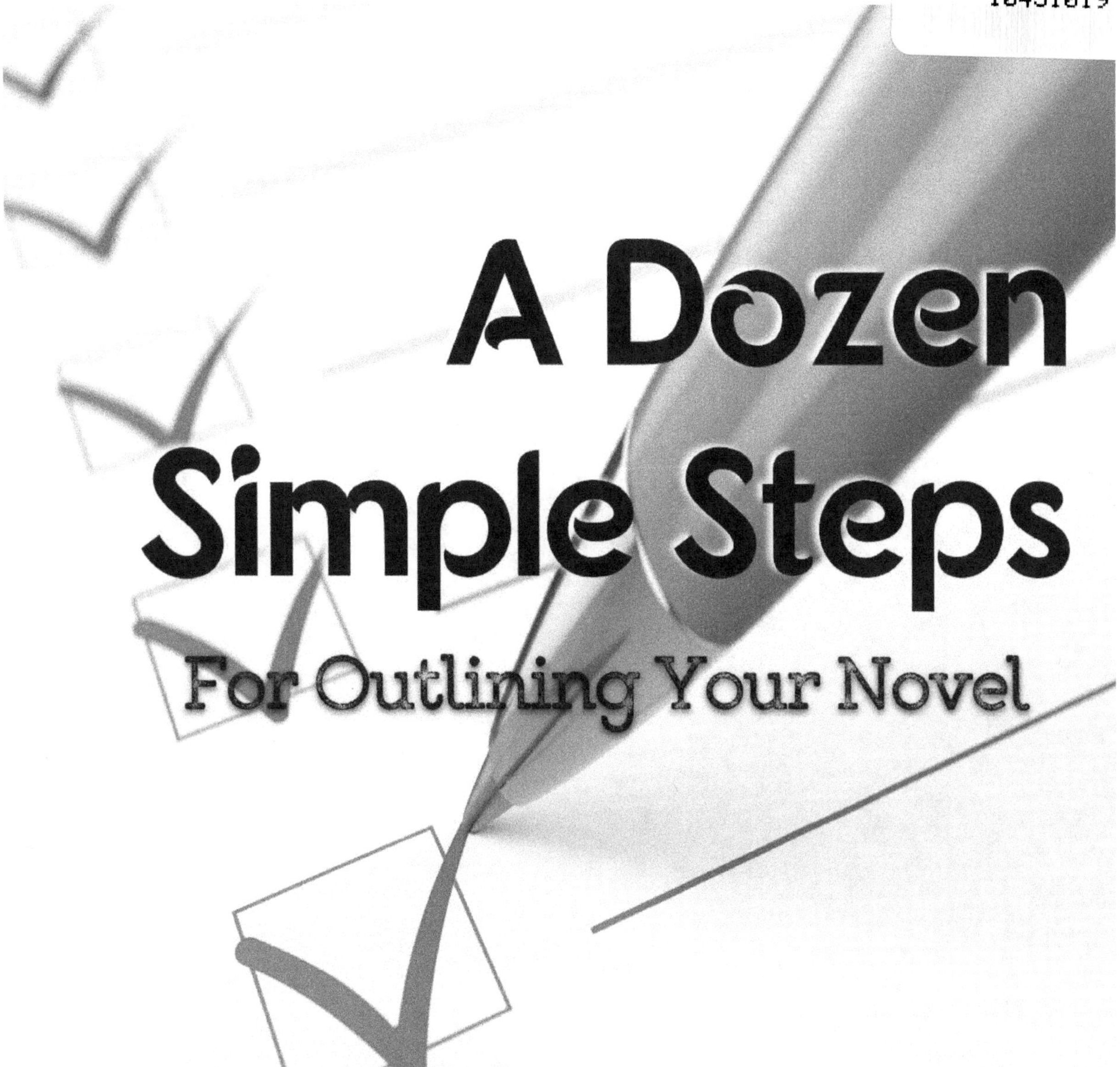

A Dozen Simple Steps

For Outlining Your Novel

A Simple Yet Effective Way To Go From Idea To Complete Storyline

A Liar's Craft Product

ISBN: 978-0-9836270-4-3
Printed in the USA

Cover & Interior Design By: www.TheLiarsCraft.com

INTRODUCTION

Are you the type of person that just sits down and starts typing when an idea comes into your head? You're really pounding on that keyboard and before you know it it's time to read over what your blood, sweat and tears put on that paper. You are reading along, big smile on your face, and then you realize something is missing. There's a hole. A plot hole! How did you miss it? How are you going to fix it?

Being a pantser can be exciting, and who wants to be a boring plotter anyway? Well, being a plotter has it's advantages. By outlining your story ahead of time, you can recognize possible plot holes before it becomes a page full of red ink.

What you will learn in this workbook is a step by step guide to outlining your book in a methodical and efficient way that barely leaves room for potholes. The steps are easy to understand and implement. There are many ways to outline a story and this workbook will show you one of many. But ultimately you should use the method that works best for you in creating a quality masterpiece.

Step 1: The Title Page

Here you will record your book title, the date you started, completed and published your project as well as the genre.

BOOK TITLE:

____

____

DATE STARTED:

____

DATE COMPLETED:

____

DATE PUBLISHED:

____

GENRE:

Step 2: Book Overview

Use this section to write a brief description of your novel. It can be include basic information such as who, what, where, when and why. It should be reminiscent of a synopsis.

BOOK OVERVIEW:

Step 3: Who

In this section you will list your characters and their role in the story. (Antagonist, Protagonist or side-kick)

Who

(Antagonist, Protagonist, Side-kicks, ect)

Step 4: What

What do your characters want? What are their attitudes toward each other? Are they friends or foe?

What

(A few sentences to describe your book)

Step 5: When/Where

This section is about the location and place in time your story takes place. Is it present day in an actual real life location? Does it take place in the past or future? Does it take place in a fictional city or a world you created?

When/Where

(Era Story Takes Place/Scene List)

Step 6: Why

What is your main character's motivation? What drives him/her?

Why

(Main Character's Motivation)

Step 7: Plotline

Here is where you flesh out a more detailed outline for your project. What is the majority of your story about? What pushes the story forward. What is the main plot of the story? What trials will the characters have to overcome? Will they overcome them?

Plotline

(What's it about)

Step 8: Subplot #1

What else is going on? Most stories aren't just focused on one thing. Our lives are made up of many stories going on at once that is unrelated to our main objection.. An example may be a falling out with a friend that needs to be resolved before the end of the story.

Subplot #1

(What else is going on?)

step 9: subplot #2

This is the same as subplot #1, however it should be a different issue fallen upon a different character.

What else is going on? Most stories aren't just focused on one thing. Our lives are made up of many stories going on at once that is unrelated to our main objection.. An example may be a falling out with a friend that needs to be resolved before the end of the story.

Subplot #2

(What else is going on? Something different.)

Step 10: Minor Plot Twist

Something unexpected goes here. It's not a huge deal but it is something the reader did not see coming and could possibly affect the outcome of the story.

Minor Plot Twist

(Something unexpected but easily resolved happens)

Step 11: Major Plot Twist

Just like the Minor Plot Twist, except this is a HUGE deal and completely catches the reader off guard. This could be a secret revealed that completely changes the game plan and the reader's anticipated end to this story.

Major Plot Twist

(Something unexpected but maybe not so easily resolved happens)

Step 12: Resolution

How does it end? Have all the loose ends been tied up in a nice neat package? (Unless, of course, it's a series or serial.)

Resolution

(How will it end?)

Well, there you have it…

A Dozen Simple Steps For Outlining Your Novel.

Now grab that pen and

Let's get started!

BOOK TITLE:

____

DATE STARTED:

____

DATE COMPLETED:

____

DATE PUBLISHED:

____

GENRE:

BOOK OVERVIEW:

Who

(Antagonist, Protagonist, Side-kicks, ect)

What

(A few sentences to describe your book)

When/Where

(Era Story Takes Place/Scene List)

Why

(Main Character's Motivation)

Plotline

(What's it about)

Subplot #1

(What else is going on?)

Subplot #2

(What else is going on? Something different.)

Minor Plot Twist

(Something unexpected but easily resolved happens)

Major Plot Twist

(Something unexpected but maybe not so easily resolved happens)

Resolution

(How will it end?)

BOOK TITLE:

DATE STARTED:

DATE COMPLETED:

DATE PUBLISHED:

GENRE:

BOOK OVERVIEW:

Who

(Antagonist, Protagonist, Side-kicks, ect)

What

(A few sentences to describe your book)

When/Where

(Era Story Takes Place/Scene List)

Why

(Main Character's Motivation)

Plotline

(What's it about)

Subplot #1

(What else is going on?)

Subplot #2

(What else is going on? Something different.)

Minor Plot Twist

(Something unexpected but easily resolved happens)

Major Plot Twist

(Something unexpected but maybe not so easily resolved happens)

Resolution

(How will it end?)

BOOK TITLE:

DATE STARTED:

DATE COMPLETED:

DATE PUBLISHED:

GENRE:

BOOK OVERVIEW:

Who

(Antagonist, Protagonist, Side-kicks, ect)

What

(A few sentences to describe your book)

When/Where

(Era Story Takes Place/Scene List)

Why

(Main Character's Motivation)

Plotline

(What's it about)

Subplot #1

(What else is going on?)

Subplot #2

(What else is going on? Something different.)

Minor Plot Twist

(Something unexpected but easily resolved happens)

Major Plot Twist

(Something unexpected but maybe not so easily resolved happens)

Resolution

(How will it end?)

BOOK TITLE:

DATE STARTED:

DATE COMPLETED:

DATE PUBLISHED:

GENRE:

BOOK OVERVIEW:

Who

(Antagonist, Protagonist, Side-kicks, ect)

What

(A few sentences to describe your book)

When/Where

(Era Story Takes Place/Scene List)

Why

(Main Character's Motivation)

Plotline

(What's it about)

Subplot #1

(What else is going on?)

Subplot #2

(What else is going on? Something different.)

Minor Plot Twist

(Something unexpected but easily resolved happens)

Major Plot Twist

(Something unexpected but maybe not so easily resolved happens)

Resolution

(How will it end?)

BOOK TITLE:

DATE STARTED:

DATE COMPLETED:

DATE PUBLISHED:

GENRE:

BOOK OVERVIEW:

Who

(Antagonist, Protagonist, Side-kicks, ect)

What

(A few sentences to describe your book)

When/Where

(Era Story Takes Place/Scene List)

Why

(Main Character's Motivation)

Plotline

(What's it about)

Subplot #1

(What else is going on?)

Subplot #2

(What else is going on? Something different.)

Minor Plot Twist

(Something unexpected but easily resolved happens)

Major Plot Twist

(Something unexpected but maybe not so easily resolved happens)

Resolution

(How will it end?)

BOOK TITLE:

____

____

DATE STARTED:

____

DATE COMPLETED:

____

DATE PUBLISHED:

____

GENRE:

BOOK OVERVIEW:

Who

(Antagonist, Protagonist, Side-kicks, ect)

What

(A few sentences to describe your book)

When/Where

(Era Story Takes Place/Scene List)

Why

(Main Character's Motivation)

Plotline

(What's it about)

Subplot #1

(What else is going on?)

Subplot #2

(What else is going on? Something different.)

Minor Plot Twist

(Something unexpected but easily resolved happens)

Major Plot Twist

(Something unexpected but maybe not so easily resolved happens)

Resolution

(How will it end?)

BOOK TITLE:

DATE STARTED:

DATE COMPLETED:

DATE PUBLISHED:

GENRE:

BOOK OVERVIEW:

Who

(Antagonist, Protagonist, Side-kicks, ect)

What

(A few sentences to describe your book)

When/Where

(Era Story Takes Place/Scene List)

Why

(Main Character's Motivation)

Plotline

(What's it about)

Subplot #1

(What else is going on?)

Subplot #2

(What else is going on? Something different.)

Minor Plot Twist

(Something unexpected but easily resolved happens)

Major Plot Twist

(Something unexpected but maybe not so easily resolved happens)

Resolution

(How will it end?)

BOOK TITLE:

DATE STARTED:

DATE COMPLETED:

DATE PUBLISHED:

GENRE:

BOOK OVERVIEW:

Who

(Antagonist, Protagonist, Side-kicks, ect)

What

(A few sentences to describe your book)

When/Where

(Era Story Takes Place/Scene List)

Why

(Main Character's Motivation)

Plotline

(What's it about)

Subplot #1

(What else is going on?)

Subplot #2

(What else is going on? Something different.)

Minor Plot Twist

(Something unexpected but easily resolved happens)

Major Plot Twist

(Something unexpected but maybe not so easily resolved happens)

Resolution

(How will it end?)

BOOK TITLE:

DATE STARTED:

DATE COMPLETED:

DATE PUBLISHED:

GENRE:

BOOK OVERVIEW:

Who

(Antagonist, Protagonist, Side-kicks, ect)

What

(A few sentences to describe your book)

When/Where

(Era Story Takes Place/Scene List)

Why

(Main Character's Motivation)

Plotline

(What's it about)

Subplot #1

(What else is going on?)

Subplot #2

(What else is going on? Something different.)

Minor Plot Twist

(Something unexpected but easily resolved happens)

Major Plot Twist

(Something unexpected but maybe not so easily resolved happens)

Resolution

(How will it end?)

BOOK TITLE:

DATE STARTED:

DATE COMPLETED:

DATE PUBLISHED:

GENRE:

BOOK OVERVIEW:

Who

(Antagonist, Protagonist, Side-kicks, ect)

What

(A few sentences to describe your book)

When/Where

(Era Story Takes Place/Scene List)

Why

(Main Character's Motivation)

Plotline

(What's it about)

Subplot #1

(What else is going on?)

Subplot #2

(What else is going on? Something different.)

Minor Plot Twist

(Something unexpected but easily resolved happens)

Major Plot Twist

(Something unexpected but maybe not so easily resolved happens)

Resolution

(How will it end?)

BOOK TITLE:

DATE STARTED:

DATE COMPLETED:

DATE PUBLISHED:

GENRE:

BOOK OVERVIEW:

Who

(Antagonist, Protagonist, Side-kicks, ect)

What

(A few sentences to describe your book)

When/Where

(Era Story Takes Place/Scene List)

Why

(Main Character's Motivation)

Plotline

(What's it about)

Subplot #1

(What else is going on?)

Subplot #2

(What else is going on? Something different.)

Minor Plot Twist

(Something unexpected but easily resolved happens)

Major Plot Twist

(Something unexpected but maybe not so easily resolved happens)

Resolution

(How will it end?)

Notes:

www.ingramcontent.com/pod-product-compliance
Lightning Source LLC
Chambersburg PA
CBHW081146170626
46809CB00010B/3111